# Celebrating Samhain

## The Celtic Wheel of the Year

### Book 1

# RIONNA MORGAN

Celebrating Samhain
The Celtic Wheel of the Year
Book 1

Cover art and Illustrations
made by the Author
with the assistance of Midjourney

ISBN: 978-1-962668-99-6

For my children— T, C, G, M
For your children—
And for theirs—
I love you, forever.

Beloved Readers,

I hope this letter finds you just in from a stroll in the crisp fall air or better yet a scramble in after a few rowdy jumps in the leaf pile. Perhaps now you're ready to curl up with a warm cup of cider or a delicious mug of hot chocolate and bask in the soft glow of flickering candlelight.

My name is Rionna Morgan, and I am so happy to be sharing this time of year with you. As the author of *The Celtic Wheel of the Year* series, I felt compelled to share a piece of my heart with you. I was born to parents of Irish descent, raised by a single mother, and my childhood was beautifully woven with Celtic traditions, each Festival and Esbat a cherished memory. The tales, songs, and age-old rituals provided not just a sense of belonging but also a profound understanding of love and compassion in their purest forms.

It is this same warmth of memory, this unconditional love, that I sought to capture in my writing. The series was born from a place of deep reverence and affection for my roots and traditions of my youth. But beyond just a story, my most earnest aspiration is to spread love. In the world we inhabit, where days can sometimes seem bleak and disconnected, I yearn for these tales to act as a shield. By doing so I hope they protect and remind us of the boundless love that exists and can be found in the traditions we build and celebrate.

As you turn the pages, know that you aren't just journeying through a fictional tale with these beautiful characters who took pieces of this family and that family to create a single unit of love and connection. You are, in many ways, tracing the contours of my own heart, my memories, and my deepest hopes. Thank you for giving my stories a home in your heart, and in return, I send to you across the miles all the warmth and love that has inspired this series. May your home be the safest of havens, abounding with love and happiness.

All my love,
Rionna

# Celebrating Samhain

## The Celtic Wheel of the Year

## Book 1

All day Croia and Ronan were excited. They raced through their work at school. They scarfed their lunches and tried hard to actually listen to their friends at recess. They managed to ignore and escape the bully in the eighth grade who teased everybody and knocked down the little kids. They rolled their eyes – inwardly of course – when their teacher had just *one more thing to say* before she let them leave at the end of the day.

When the bell rang, they grabbed their backpacks and ran as quickly as they could – without getting into trouble – to where their sister was parked to pick them up from school. Every second of their day had been filled with the best kind of can't-wait butterflies.

"Do you think she brought us presents?" Ronan blurted as soon as he had his seatbelt buckled.

"Chocolates!" Croia squealed. "It is Halloween after all."

Croia and Ronan chattered back and forth the whole way home about all the things that could possibly be presents. They tried to get Kenna, their new sister, to join them in the conversation, but she just smiled quietly and drove.

So, the twins simply plotted and planned all the fun adventures they were looking forward to having. They clapped their hands and raced to go inside as soon as the car stopped in their driveway, calling back their thank yous for the ride as they ran.

The scent of air filled with warm cinnamon and molasses met them as they zipped up the stairs and into the kitchen.

"Grandmother!" Croia and Ronan's excited voices chimed in unison.

"My darlings!" A lady in a smart pantsuit covered by a pleated apron turned and opened her arms to envelope them.

They wrapped their arms around their grandmother and snuggled in, just like they'd done since they were little. Her long gray hair swished about them, and they breathed in scents of black currants and vanilla.

"Hooray! Finally, you're home!" their grandmother cheered. "How was your day? Tell me everything you can remember."

Before they could begin with the barrage of stories which they knew their grandmother loved, they heard someone behind them.

"Umm. Hi," the voice said. "I brought in your backpacks and hung them in the hallway." Kenna looked around and chewed on her bottom lip.

"Kenna!" Croia said as she went to stand beside her. "Thank you! We forgot. We were so excited!"

"Come meet Grandmother!" Ronan waved welcome to Kenna. "She's from Ireland."

Grandmother smiled and walked toward Kenna. "I'm Brighid Hughes." She held out her hand.

Kenna hesitated. But eventually she reached back to shake the offered hand. "I'm Kenna," she replied, her insides skittering with uneasiness.

"I'm happy to know you. We were just getting ready to have a snack and a cup of tea. Do you want to join us?"

Croia and Ronan settled themselves at the table and waited. They crossed their fingers and hoped that Kenna would come sit with them.

Kenna looked around the kitchen. She couldn't believe it was the same one she'd left this morning to go to school. The kitchen from this morning had normal stuff – the stove, the dishwasher, the pots and pans hanging on their ceiling rack, and a simply adorned dining table with only a cream cloth covering.

This kitchen, while the same, was very *very* different. Dotted along the once bare counters were loaves of bread, pumpkins, apples, squash, potatoes, and some things that looked like turnips? On the stove a deep, hearty looking stew simmered with fat carrots, meat, and potatoes.

The table now had three burning candles and was set for what she could only imagine was tea with sliced bread, little cakes, cups with saucers and small plates at each chair.

She wanted to say no and just go to her room like always, but her stomach was saying yes. She wasn't comfortable enough to eat lunch at her new school and everything on the table looked so good. She could see Croia and Ronan watching her with eager, hopeful eyes.

"Sure," she said quietly and jumped in her skin a bit when Croia and Ronan cheered.

The four of them sat together to share the afterschool snack. Ronan and Croia took turns telling stories about their day, making Grandmother gasp and laugh. They tried to coax Kenna to share about her day, but she wouldn't. They asked Grandmother about her flight across the ocean, about the food on the plane, and how long the trip took.

"Grandmother, do you really get to stay all year?" Ronan asked between bites of cake and sips of tea.

"Yes, dearie, I do. If you'll have me." Grandmother smiled.

Croia grinned and asked, "Is it really a tradition in our family?"

"Yes, it is." Grandmother served another piece of brown soda bread to Kenna and filled her cup with more tea. "Every year when a grandchild turns 12, the matriarch grandmother goes to spend a year with the child's family."

"Why?" Ronan asked.

"To spend time with them when they are old enough to remember, so they can look back when they are grown. To be with them before they get wrapped up in all the planning and dreaming of their future. To help them learn at an age that still glimmers with a bit of childhood magic, but also shows glimpses of who they will grow to become."

"Huh!?" Ronan gaped.

Grandmother laughed and hugged him.

"I think she means that she wants to spend time with us before we get too big," Croia said.

Grandmother nodded and sipped her tea.

"Am I too big?" Kenna blurted before she could stop herself.

"Not at all!" Grandmother reached and patted Kenna's hand. "We are all going to have a beautiful year!"

"You said you are here to teach us stuff. What stuff?" Ronan reached for another cake.

"The song of our family. And some other stuff. I have a whole list." Grandmother winked.

The clock on the wall chimed the hour, and Grandmother stood up from her chair.

"It's time," she said.

"For what?" the three asked nearly in unison.

"To start on that list. Would you like to help me?" Grandmother asked.

"Yes!" they answered.

"Okay. Let's tidy up, and then we'll get started."

Each of them helped clear the table, wrap the cakes and bread, and load the dishwasher.

"Let's grab that and go outside." Grandmother pointed to a large basket tucked beside the stove.

Kenna picked it up and followed everyone to the backyard.

They hadn't lived in this house for very long, just since the beginning of the school year. The backyard was already their favorite place. It meandered down a small hill, and there were a few steps that led the way to where the flat ground, covered with wild grass, spread out wide and open.

Winding through the grass there was a path that was perfect for taking walks down to the little creek that wove its way through the border of their two acres. Around the edges of the yard was a wooden fence with birdhouses perched here and there. A poplar tree stood very tall with branches that swayed in the breeze.

Kenna's dad, when he wasn't working at the university in town, liked to explore the woods along the creek. He was always finding rocks to pick up to show everyone. He was a geology professor and loved rocks. There was a big pile of them at the base of the poplar tree – *my collection*, he'd say and laugh.

A little further away from the base of the tree was a long wooden picnic table with benches on each side. This belonged to Croia and Ronan. Their father made it for them, when they were two, right before he left for the war in Afghanistan. But he died and never got to come home. Knowing this, and that they wouldn't ever get to sit at it with him, tugged at Kenna's heart. Every time she looked at it, she felt a pang of sadness.

She knew what it felt like to lose a parent. Except her mother wasn't dead. She was just gone. She left when Kenna was three and never came back. That was thirteen years ago. Kenna didn't even remember her, and it had been years since she stopped asking her dad about her. It always seemed to make him sad. He'd slump his shoulders and bow his head anytime she brought her up. So, Kenna stopped doing it.

Now though, her dad was never sad like that. He smiled practically all the time since he met and married Croia and Ronan's mom. Kenna liked Maeve well enough. She was a nurse and liked to tell jokes. She was never cross with her, not like some of the other moms the kids at school talked about. She was patient. She would look at Kenna with eyes that seemed like she was waiting for something.

"Kenna!" Ronan called from across the yard.

"Grandmother says we get to build a fire."

"Oh yeah?" Kenna replied, setting the basket on the picnic table. "Really?"

"Really," Grandmother said. "But first I have a story."

"Okay," Croia said, sitting next to Kenna and looping arms with her.

Kenna still wasn't used to her new siblings. She wasn't used to Ronan and Croia's loud chatter, their echoing laughter, or the way they danced in the kitchen to random songs from the radio. She liked it. They made her laugh. They made her heart feel warm.

Especially when Croia would come up and hold her hand or loop her arm through hers like she was doing now. But she felt a little bit like an outsider. And she still jumped when Croia yelled across the yard to Ronan.

"Story time!"

Grandmother waited until everyone was settled at the table before she began to speak.

"What day is it today?" Grandmother asked.

"Halloween!" Ronan called out the answer.

"That's right." Grandmother smiled and patted his hand. "How do you celebrate Halloween?"

"We dress up in costumes, carve pumpkins, and go trick-or-treating," Croia replied.

"That is also correct." Grandmother patted her hand. "Do you know that I celebrate Halloween too?"

"You do?" Kenna puzzled.

"I do." Grandmother smiled and noticed Kenna's surprised frown. "I would like to share how I grew up celebrating it and invite you all to celebrate with me. If you want to."

"Okay!" Croia said and squeezed Kenna's arm with excitement.

"Is this one of the things on your list?" Ronan asked.

"It is," Grandmother replied.

"Okay then," Ronan smiled as he answered.

Grandmother looked to Kenna.

Kenna recognized the waiting look, the patient look, and almost smiled at how familiar it seemed.

But she just nodded her head and tried not to appear skeptical.

"When I was growing up, when my own grandmother came the year I turned 12, she taught me about Halloween and how it has been celebrated by the Celtic people for more than 2,000 years."

"Two thousand years!" Ronan exclaimed.

"Celtic people?" Croia asked.

"People who live in Ireland, Scotland, Wales and the surrounding areas," Kenna answered. "We learned about them in history class a little."

"Wonderful! Very good. That's right," Grandmother replied. "Halloween started in Ireland. But instead of Halloween, it's called Samhain." Grandmother leaned in and formed the word again, saying, "It's pronounced saw win."

Grandmother waited until everyone practiced saying the word before continuing. "We dress up in costumes too. We carve turnips in place of pumpkins. We visit neighbors and exchange sweet treats. We play games, have a special dinner, and we build a fire." She tipped her head toward Ronan.

"Yes!" He clapped his hands.

"Anyone have any guesses why we do all these things?" Grandmother asked and smiled as she waited for their answers.

What a picture they make, she thought. Everyone was leaning forward. Their eyes wide and a little excited.

Kenna's black hair wisped across her face, but she didn't brush it away. Ronan's elbows were on the table with his chin propped up in his hands. Croia squeezed Kenna's arm. They all just waited.

"We do all these things to honor and remember the people we love who have died," Grandmother said.

"Like Grandfather?" Croia asked in a quiet voice.

"Like Dad?" Ronan asked.

"Yes." Grandmother reached across the table to hold their hands. "We believe that on Samhain, the veil between our worlds is thinnest, and that the spirits of our loved ones can walk among us. They can hear us, be with us, and comfort us. To honor their visit, we set a place at our table for them to come eat with us." Grandmother motioned down the length of the table. "Our burning candles and special fire light the way for them to find us."

"Can we do that?" Croia asked. Her voice cracked as tears slipped down her cheeks.

"Yes, we can do that," Grandmother answered.

"Can we do that for people who aren't here now, but maybe are still living?" Kenna asked, thinking of her mother.

Grandmother nodded. "Of course."

"What do we do first?" Ronan asked, his voice thick with emotion.

"How about we set the table and prepare for our bonfire?" Grandmother answered and pulled him close to her.

After a few moments each of them stood to begin. They gathered rocks from the collection beneath the poplar tree to make a fire circle. As they worked, Grandmother continued her stories about Samhain, telling them more about how it's the Celtic New Year, and that the costumes and the gnarled faces in the carved turnips protect them from evil spirits. She talked to them about gathering wood for the fire and that with each stick they could send a message or a wish to a loved one. She explained that their feelings of love and care would be delivered by the smoke as the fire burned.

They worked in silence for the most part. Each of them lost in their own thoughts with the crisp fall winds swirling around them. They dug into Grandmother's basket and found the tablecloth and candles. They covered the table with the long dark cloth and placed the candles in the center. Kenna and Croia ran up to the house to get plates, bowls, and silverware for the table. Kenna stopped in her room to get a framed picture of her mother. Croia took a picture of her father in his Army uniform off the table in the hallway.

Everyone made several more trips back and forth to the house getting everything they would need for dinner, the traditional Barm Brack bread, the apple cinnamon cake, and the basket of apples. They all paused to put on their costumes and to cheer at how wonderful everyone looked. They even carved a few turnips. Everything was ready. Dusk began to settle around them with the peaceful chill of fall.

They sat together at the long table. The candles burned, their flames flickering in the gentle evening breeze. There were nine places set, each with a plate, a bowl, a napkin, silverware, and a heavy mug. Beside Grandmother was the plate she'd set for her husband.

"Kenna," Grandmother spoke gently and pointed to the basket that had held the candles and the tablecloth. "There is a picture of Grandfather in there. Will you bring it to me please?"

Kenna nodded her head and pulled the picture free. "There is a small blanket in here. Do we need that too?"

"We may need it yet. We'll wait and see." Grandmother took the picture Kenna handed her and set it just above the plate where Grandfather would have sat beside her. "Thank you, Kenna," she said, her voice a little heavy with sadness.

Ronan and Croia saw this and placed the picture of their father above the place they'd set for him. Kenna did the same with the picture of her mother. All together their hearts felt full of memories, wished-for memories, and the sadness of loss.

"It's nice to be here together," Grandmother said as they all settled in their seats.

"It's nice to remember." Kenna bowed her head.

"I feel like he might be sitting here with us." Ronan held his sister's hand as her eyes filled, and she nodded her head yes.

This is how Maeve and Tate found them. Maeve's heart filled with such emotion of peace and love as she took in the scene below. Her mother sat with her children, all three of them, and their rambunctious, busy selves were quiet, seated together, and honoring their loved ones with such sacred reverence. Her breath caught and she squeezed her husband's hand.

"Let's go join them." Tate smiled and helped her down the steps to the yard.

"Hello, my lovelies," Maeve called.

"Mom!" Ronan and Croia cried in unison.

"Look what we did!" Croia chimed, motioning to the table.

Kenna was startled, but then she laughed aloud with all the excitement.

Tate went to stand near Kenna. "Didn't you have a Halloween party with your friends tonight?"

"I texted them to let them know we had family visiting," Kenna answered.

"That is very kind." Maeve smiled and smoothed her hand across Kenna's back. "Thank you."

"And Grandmother said we could have a fire!" Ronan cheered and hugged his mom. "When do we get to light it?" he asked Grandmother.

"After dinner." Grandmother laughed.

"Then let's eat!" Ronan motioned to the table with his hands.

"Tate, would you and Kenna get the stew and hot apple cider off the stove, please?" Grandmother asked.

"Sure!" Tate and Kenna headed to the house.

"I'll cut the bread," Maeve said.

When Tate and Kenna returned, Ronan and Croia cheered, and everyone settled around the table.

Grandmother ladled the stew and served the bread. Kenna poured the hot spiced cider. Maeve hinted that they might find surprises in the Barm Brack bread that would bring them good luck in the coming year. Everyone dug through their slices and called out their discoveries. Maeve told them the meaning of each trinket or bead they found, as Tate passed around the honey butter.

Between mouthfuls of stew and bites of bread, they all chattered about their day. Kenna told her dad what she'd learned about Samhain and how long it had been celebrated by the Celtic people. Grandmother told some of the old stories about Lady Gwen, the fairies, pookas, and headless men on horses until everyone's imaginations were running wild.

The music of their laughter and happy voices drifted beyond the table, beyond the reach of the candlelight, and out into the night. Every once in a while, they would pause to look at the empty seats at the table. Amidst feeling a wistful sense of sadness, they also felt sparks of gratitude and peace in honoring their loved ones.

As the stories continued, Grandmother taught them how to play an apple game to see who could peel an apple with the longest unbroken strand of peel. Then they took turns throwing the long peeling over their left shoulder to see what shape it made when it landed. Grandmother told them about the old belief, that the peeling shapes could tell the future of the coming year. They laughed at how tricky it was to actually do, and they cheered for each other as the peelings kept getting longer and longer.

"You have a knack for this." Maeve smiled as she pointed to Kenna's most recent peeling toss.

"Your year is going to be filled with all sorts of things, it seems." Grandmother patted Kenna's knee.

"Yeah!" Ronan counted off on his fingers. "A car, a crown, a trophy."

"Geez!" Kenna laughed.

"A cat!" Croia called out. "This one looks like a cat."

The game continued as Grandmother served the apple cinnamon cake with everyone yelling out what shapes their apple peels landed in. She drizzled each piece with a custard cream sauce and whispered quietly in Ronan's ear.

"It's time to light the fire."

"Really?" he whispered back. His eyes grew wide.

Grandmother nodded and was surprised when he didn't jump and cheer as he had before.

Instead, he simply asked, "Dad will be able to find us then?"

"Let's find out." Grandmother hugged him, and she smiled when he hugged her back.

Everyone finished the last bites of their cake and hung their apple peelings on the nearby tree branches for the birds.

Maeve and Tate gathered a few more sticks for the fire to add their own good wishes. Croia and Kenna placed old stumps around the circle for everyone to sit on. Grandmother and Ronan knelt down and started the fire.

"Oh," Tate said. "You used my rocks for the ring." He smiled and held out his hand to Kenna.

"That's lovely." Maeve reached to hold Tate's other hand.

"It was Kenna's idea," Croia said as she took ahold of Kenna's hand and reached for Grandmother's.

Grandmother smiled and gathered Ronan's hand in hers. She nodded toward Maeve and Ronan pulled his mother's hand into his.

As they formed their circle around the fire, the air stilled, and the gentle wind paused. Their ringing laughter and cheering from before fell quiet and settled to a joyful silence in their hearts. The flames flickered, casting their golden light. The fire burned, sending their messages of love as sparks and smoke up into the darkness. The full moon shone high in the sky, veiling the midnight shadows with a glimmer of silver.

"Do you hear that?" Kenna asked.

Everyone listened.

"I don't—," Tate responded.

"Sshh. There it is again."

Kenna let go of the hands she was holding and ran toward the creek bed. "It sounds like crying," she yelled back.

"You all stay here," Tate said, his voice firm as he followed Kenna.

Kenna and Tate's voices drifted out of hearing distance. The others waited, holding hands, looking beyond the firelight.

Minutes passed. But soon they could see Tate and Kenna walking back toward them. It looked like Kenna was carrying something in her arms.

"What is it, Mom?" Croia asked.

"I don't know, honey," answered Maeve. "Let's just wait and see."

"Ronan." Grandmother motioned to the basket they brought down earlier. "Why don't you go get that. We might need it."

Ronan hurried over and brought it back. He took ahold of Grandmother's hand and waited.

"Look what we found," Kenna said at almost a whisper as she entered the ring of firelight.

She leaned down and opened her arms. Tucked in her hands was a small black kitten.

"Oh my." Maeve pulled a stump closer to the fire. "Here, sit here."

Kenna settled onto the stump, and everyone gathered around her.

"He's all wet!" Croia croaked out a strained whisper.

"Where did you find him?" Ronan asked in a low voice.

"He was hanging onto a branch in the creek," Tate said, pulling another stump over to sit beside Kenna.

"Grandmother," Kenna said. "Do we still have that small blanket?"

"Yes, dearie." Grandmother pulled the blanket from the basket and helped Kenna wrap the furry little baby with the warm, soft cloth.

Maeve and Tate looked at each other over Grandmother and Kenna's bent heads, sending a wordless message. Maeve squeezed her eyes shut and grinned. Tate linked his fingers with hers and smiled.

Ronan and Croia had seen that look on their mom's face a million times. It was her I'm-so-happy-I-could-cry look. The twins glanced at Grandmother and Kenna and back at each other. Then they smiled, sending silent messages of their own.

Ronan and Croia pulled a stump closer for Grandmother to sit next to Kenna. The kitten was curled up in the blanket with only its little face showing. Its big eyes gazed up at them and blinked as Kenna smoothed her fingers over the little ears.

"Such long blinks," Maeve said as she smoothed her hand over Kenna's hair.

"A sleepy fellow," Croia said.

"A little sandman." Kenna nodded.

They gathered together around Kenna and the kitten. The quiet of the night settled in. The golden light and silver shadows of Samhain enveloped them. They could feel the comfort come.

They could feel the solace of their sacred memories. They could feel the love of those who were not with them, just at the edges of the fire's glow.

Kenna began to rock back and forth and hum a little under her breath.

"It's the song of our family." Ronan smiled looking at Grandmother, remembering their earlier conversation.

"What's the song of our family?" Croia asked.

"Love," Kenna responded and leaned toward her family who wrapped their arms around her and each other.

# Samhain
## Recipes

# Barm Brack

4 cups of flour

1/2 teaspoon of cinnamon

1/4 teaspoon of nutmeg

1/2 teaspoon of salt

2 heaping tablespoons of butter

1 package of yeast

1 cup sugar, divided

1 cup warm milk, divided

1 egg

1 1/2 cup of golden raisins

1 cup currants

1/2 cup, mixed candied peel

*Assorted beads and trinkets: various colored beads, ring, coin, stick, pea, thimble, each individually wrapped in waxed paper.*

Sift together the flour, spices, and salt: pinch or rub in butter with fingers. Cream the yeast with 1 teaspoon of the sugar and 1 teaspoon warm milk; mixture should froth up. If it doesn't it means the yeast is old. Add the remaining sugar to the flour mixture and blend well. Pour the remaining milk and the egg into the yeast mixture and combine with the flour mixture. Beat well with a wooden spoon. The batter should be stiff, but elastic. Fold in fruit, chopped peel, and wrapped divination pieces (beads and trinkets).

Cover with a cloth and leave in a warm place until dough doubles in size. Turn out and divide into 2 loaves. Place each loaf in a greased 7-inch cake tin. Cover again and let rise for about 30 minutes. Bake at 400 degrees for 1 hour. Test with a skewer before removing from oven. Glaze with 1 tablespoon of sugar dissolved in 2 teaspoons boiling water and return to oven for 3 minutes.

Turn out onto rack to cool. Slice and serve with butter or honey butter: equal parts of honey and softened butter mixed.

*From Rionna: This is a favorite recipe that I make in our home on Samhain. It comes from CELTIC COOKING Asala, J. (1998). Celtic Folklore Cooking. Llewellyn Worldwide.*

# Irish Stew

3 pounds of lamb or *beef*\*
2 pounds of potatoes
*2 pounds of carrots*\*
1 pound of onions
1/2 tablespoon chopped parsley
1/2 tablespoon fresh thyme
2 cups water
Salt and pepper to taste

*\*Traditional Irish Stew is made with lamb. My family likes beef, so I substitute that in. I also add carrots; I like them too!*

Cut meat into pieces. (Brown in hot skillet if using beef). Peel and chop potatoes, carrots, and onions. Layer half of the potatoes in saucepan, then half of the meat and herbs, and finally half of the onion and carrots. Season each layer to taste and repeat the process.

Pour water over, cover with a sheet of foil as well as the lid, and simmer gently for about 2 hours, occasionally shaking the pan to prevent sticking. Add liquid if it seems too dry, but a good Irish stew should be thick and not like a soup.

*From Rionna: This is a favorite recipe that I make in our home on Samhain. It comes from CELTIC COOKING Asala, J. (1998). Celtic Folklore Cooking. Llewellyn Worldwide.*

# Apple Cake

## Cake

2 eggs
1 plus 1/2 cup of sugar
1/3 cup of cream
1 stick butter, softened
    Pinch of salt
1 apple, peeled, cored, and grated

1 1/2 cups of flour
1 1/2 teaspoons of baking powder
1 1/2 teaspoons of freshly ground cinnamon
4 medium apples, peeled, cored, and sliced

Beat the eggs with 1 cup of sugar. Combine cream, butter, and salt in a small saucepan. Heat until near boiling. Remove and immediately pour onto the egg mixture. Fold in the grated apple, flour, baking powder, and cinnamon. Pour the batter into a greased 9 x 9 inch baking pan. Arrange the apple slices on top and sprinkle with the remaining sugar or a streusel topping. Bake for about 20 minutes at 400 degrees, or until cake is firm to the touch. Serve warm with a cream sauce - I've included my favorite one below.

*From Rionna: This is a favorite recipe that I make in our home on Samhain. It comes from CELTIC COOKING Asala, J. (1998). Celtic Folklore Cooking. Llewellyn Worldwide.*

## Cream Sauce - Family Recipe

5 or 6 large egg yolks
6 tablespoons of brown sugar

1 1/2 cup of half and half
1/2 teaspoon of vanilla

Heat half and half in a saucepan until steaming but not boiling. Whisk egg yolks and brown sugar in a bowl until pale and thick. Gradually whisk the hot milk into the yolk mixture, then return it to the saucepan. Heat while whisking until it thickens, coating the spoon. Remove from heat, add vanilla, and serve warm over cake.

# Family Recipe

INGREDIENTS:

DIRECTIONS:

# Family Recipe

INGREDIENTS:

DIRECTIONS:

# Family Recipe

INGREDIENTS:                    DIRECTIONS:

# Family Recipe

INGREDIENTS:

DIRECTIONS:

# Your Loved One

*Photos*

## A favorite memory...

_____
_____
_____
_____
_____
_____
_____
_____
_____

# Your Loved One

Photos

## A favorite memory...

_____
_____
_____
_____
_____
_____
_____
_____

# Your Loved One

Photos

## A favorite memory...

_____
_____
_____
_____
_____
_____
_____
_____
_____

# Your Loved One

Photos

## A favorite memory...

_____
_____
_____
_____
_____
_____
_____
_____
_____

www.ingramcontent.com/pod-product-compliance
Lightning Source LLC
Chambersburg PA
CBHW082132060726
47506CB00014B/1198